THE BIKER'S SECOND CHANCE

UNDERGROUND CROWS MC BOOK FOUR

SADIE KING

THE BIKER'S SECOND CHANCE

UNDERGROUND CROWS MC

Does everyone really deserve a second chance?

Of all the people to walk into the clubhouse, it had to be Sean bloody O'Leary.

He left seven years ago and broke my heart so bad I swore I'd never let a man get close to me again.

Now here he is in the flesh, with his cocky smile and Irish lilt. My body's reacting to him before my mind can shut it down.

He's begging me for a second chance, but there's no way I'm giving myself to Sean O'Leary.

No way.

But when he learns the truth of what really happened seven years ago, it might just break his heart too.

The Biker's Second Chance is an MC-lite second-chance romance featuring an OTT obsessed biker and the curvy woman he never stopped loving.

Cover designed by Designrans.

www.authorsadieking.com

1
GINA

I scrape the empty food into the trash and slam the plate into the sink. Water splashes onto the counter, and a chip of porcelain flies off the plate as it splits in two.

"Damnit."

The sink's full of water and I plunge my hand in, fishing around for the broken pieces. My finger nicks something sharp, and I jerk my hand out of the water. Blood oozes out of a small cut.

"God damnit."

This night couldn't get any worse.

Sucking on the end of my finger, I yank the plug out with my other hand. But I pull the damn thing too hard, sending more water cascading over the edge of the sink to slop onto the floor.

"Mother fucker..."

I don't usually curse this much, but then I don't usually have ghosts from my past turning up to dinner.

Of all the people to walk in the clubhouse door, it had to be Sean bloody O'Leary.

Now I'm all flustered and annoyed and doing stupid things like breaking plates and cutting myself and splashing water all over the kitchen.

I'm down on my knees mopping up with a dishcloth when the kitchen door swings open.

By the way the hairs on the back of my neck stand upright, I know it's Sean.

I stand up immediately, knocking my hip painfully against the edge of a cupboard. But damned if I'm going to be on my knees for my first encounter with Sean O'Leary in seven years.

"Hello Gina."

My name said in his Irish lilt makes my knees feel weak, and I grip the kitchen counter for support. It's beyond annoying that after all these years he can still make me weak in the knees like some giddy schoolgirl.

But I'm not a schoolgirl. I'm a thirty-three-year-old woman, and I'm not going to let this man have the satisfaction of knowing the effect he's having on me.

"Hello Sean."

I plaster on a smile that I hope gives nothing away about my thumping heart and the weak knee situation.

The bleeding's stopped in my finger, and I retrieve the broken plate and toss it in the trash.

Plates are piled up on the counter after the club

dinner, and I make myself busy rinsing dishes and loading up the dishwasher. It gives me something to do rather than look at his annoyingly handsome face.

"How have you been?" he asks casually, as if it's been a few days since we saw each other and not seven years.

"I've been good, Sean, and you?" If he wants to play it casual, fine. Two can play at that game.

"Yeah, yeah, I've been good."

I bend over to get the dishwashing detergent from under the sink.

"You look as good as I remember."

I straighten up abruptly when I realize that he's checking out my substantial ass.

I've always been a big girl, but in the last seven years I finally gave into my weight. If I crave chocolate cake, I eat it. If I want to eat ice cream straight out of the carton while watching Desperate Housewives or wherever, I do.

Because seven years ago, I made a pact with myself. I would never, ever let a man hurt me again. And with that came a sense of freedom. I no longer try to look a certain way to please a man. I do what I want, I eat what I want, and I don't give a damn what clothing size I am.

And Sean O'Leary checking out my ass is not going to change that.

I turn to face him, and he's leaning casually on the doorframe.

The years have been kind to Sean. His dark hair is peppered with silver. There are lines around his mouth and crinkles at the edges of his eyes highlighting the fact that he's spent a lifetime smiling. His beard is longer and scruffier in an endearingly rugged kind of way, and his lips are just as full and kissable as I remember.

He catches me looking at his lips, and they turn up in a cocky smile.

It's like he knows exactly what I'm thinking. Like he always did.

I pull my eyes away from him and turn the dishwasher on.

"You look the same."

It's a lie. Sean must be nearly forty now, and the years look good on him. He's got a calmness about him, a dignity that wasn't there before. Sean was always a good-looking man, but now he's downright devastating.

My stomach's tying itself up in knots, and it feels like a cage of butterflies are beating against my chest. And deep down in my core, there's a stirring that I haven't felt in a long time. Seven years to be exact.

"Are you back for a visit or for good?"

I try to sound casual, hoping he can't tell my body's gone into overdrive at the sight of him.

"It depends."

Of course it does. Sean was never one to make a commitment. I should know. We were together for two years, and he never proposed. I should have known he would leave me one day. But it was still a hell of a shock when it happened the way that it did.

I don't even bother to ask what it depends on. Probably some club business that I don't know about. The best I can do is try to stay out of his way while he's here and hope like hell he goes back to Ireland quickly.

"You never answered my letters," he says quietly.

I pause halfway through scrubbing out a pot. Sean walked out of my life seven years ago. Admittedly those were extreme circumstances, but he didn't even say goodbye.

"No," I say simply. "I didn't."

"How come, Gina? Why didn't you ever write me back?"

I rest the pot on the drying rack and turn to face him. The cocky grin has been replaced by a serious look with something like yearning.

There was a time when I was so angry at Sean that I used to imagine all the things I'd say to him when I saw him again. But now that he's here in front of me, I don't feel angry. I just feel tired.

"You left me, Sean. Did you really expect me to respond to your letters?"

His face falls.

"I never meant to hurt you, Gina. You know I would have stayed if I could."

It comes out soft as an Irish breeze, and I remember the way he used to whisper sweet nothings in my ear as we made love, driving me wild with his accent and his hot breath on my skin.

Whatever happened between us, whatever we both regret, it was a long time ago.

"It doesn't matter, Sean. We really don't need to drag

it all up. There was a time when I would have done anything for closure. But now, do you know what, Sean? I just don't care."

He stares at me for a long moment.

"I don't think that's true, love." His eyes sparkle as he takes a step towards me. "I think underneath that voluptuous, mouthwatering chest of yours, your old heart still beats for me."

Only Sean could be so crass and so romantic all in the same sentence, and only Sean could see through me so utterly.

I wipe my hands on the dishcloth and discard it on the drying rack.

"You're mistaken," I lie.

My heart's banging in my chest, and every nerve in my body is firing. I hope to God it doesn't show. I do not want to give this man the satisfaction of being right.

"I really don't care why you're back or how long you're staying. Let's just agree to stay out of each other's way, and we'll be fine."

He gives me another cocky grin. "I'm not agreeing to stay out of your way, Gina. You're too pretty to look at."

I roll my eyes. Sean was always a charmer, and nothing's changed.

"I'm done in here." Meaning with the kitchen clean up and done with this conversation.

"I'll give you a ride home on the back of my bike."

A memory flashes into my mind. Cruising down the highway. Gripping Sean's waist with my chest pressed into his back, my hair blowing in the wind. Young and in love and carefree. Stupidly thinking that this would be my forever.

"No thanks." I shake the memory out of my head. That was two different people a lifetime ago. "Not necessary. I'm having work done on my bathroom, so I'm staying at the clubhouse tonight."

"Now that's a coincidence." Sean cocks his head, a cocky sparkle in his eyes. "I'm staying here too."

My mouth drops open before I can stop myself. "You are not."

"Yes, I am, as it happens. Bruno insisted. I've already dumped my stuff in the last room on the right."

It's the room next to mine that's joined by a shared bathroom. This couldn't get any worse. But I can't let Sean see now much it bothers me.

"Just stay out of my way, Sean, and we'll be fine."

I push past him and out of the kitchen, hoping that he doesn't hear the hammering of my heart as I pass by.

Sean O'Leary is staying in the room next to mine. The man who broke my heart so badly I swore off all men. The man who still makes my insides twist and my core tighten.

I'm so fucked.

2
SEAN

The next day my mind's still on Gina. How good she looks after all these years.

She's even curvier than when I left, with a mouth-watering booty that I'd love to get my hands on. Sure, there are creases around her eyes that weren't there before, but God damn that woman is a sight for sore eyes.

I knew she wouldn't be pleased to see me, but I didn't expect that level of coolness.

I never meant to leave her the way that I did. But the circumstances were something that I couldn't control.

I thought I could explain it in the letters, but she sent every one of them back unopened. After a while I gave up, telling myself it was the best thing for her. I didn't know if I'd ever be able to come back to the States and I didn't want her to wait for me, for something I might not be able to give her.

I expected her to move on, as much as I hated the thought of it. Gina always wanted a load of kids, and I'm sad that hasn't happened for her. But also relived. The jealous bastard in me can't stand the thought of her being with anyone else.

I'm nursing a cup of coffee in the clubhouse the next morning when Bruno sits down opposite me. He slides me a bacon sandwich and bites into one of his own.

"Are you back for good?" he asks between mouthfuls.

It's just like Bruno to get down to business, no small talk.

"I hope so."

The club was my life before I left the States, and I hate that I had to leave it behind the way that I did. I missed it almost as much as I missed Gina.

I fill Bruno in on what I've been up to. We stayed in touch over the years, so he knows that I got a fake identity and tracked my mother down in Cork, helping her run the family business.

But as soon as I heard it was safe to come back to the States, I took the first plane here.

"There's always a place for you with the club if you want it." Bruno says. "I'll speak with the guys, but I know you'll be voted back in."

Bruno brings me up to speed with what the club's been up to, the legitimate strip club business and their troubles keeping drugs out of the territory.

He catches me up on what my MC brother's have been up to and the new old ladies around the club.

It turns out I'm not the only brother that had to leave in a hurry. He tells me about Ronan whose actions might have started a turf war. How he had to leave by sea the night a storm rolled. They all thought he was dead until he turned up with the local tarot reader at a caravan park in Temptation Bay.

He shows me pictures of his wife and kids on his phone. It's hard to imagine the wild Bruno I knew seven years ago settled down as a family man. But he seems happy enough. More than happy. He's beaming as he tells me about Scarlett and the audacious way he kidnapped her from a rival clubhouse.

As he's scrolling through his phone, it stops on a photo of a young woman. She's curvy with long auburn hair and bright green eyes.

"She's a beauty."

I realize my mistake as soon as I've said it.

Bruno shoves his chair back and grabs my shoulder, his fingers digging into my collarbone.

"That's my fucking daughter, man."

"That's Lily?"

When I left, Lily was an awkward adolescent, all gangly legs and braces. "I'm sorry, man, I didn't mean anything by it. All I mean is that she's grown into a lovely young woman."

He grunts at me but loosens his grip.

"Don't get any ideas, O'Leary. She's off limits."

Its goes without saying. You'd be a fool to mess around with the Pres's daughter. Bruno may have settled into family life, but he still presses iron most days by the looks of him.

"I didn't mean anything by it, Pres."

He narrows his eyes at me, still suspicious, but he sits back down.

What would I want with a young girl like that when there's a woman like Gina around? Which brings me to what I really want to talk to Bruno about.

"So, Gina's no one's old lady?" My fist clenches under the table, afraid of the answer I'm going to get.

"No."

Relief floods me, and tension eases out of my body. As much as I told myself I wanted Gina to move on, I'm so fucking glad she didn't.

"She's not met anyone then?"

Bruno gives me a hard look.

"No, not since you left."

He must see the relief on my face, but it only seems to make him tense.

"Gina was broken up after you left, Sean. Like really heartbroken."

A sharp pain tugs at my heart. I never meant to do that to Gina. I hate that I'm responsible for causing her pain.

"I had to leave. You of all people should know that."

"I know, and Gina knew why you left. But that didn't make it any easier for her."

"I want to make things right with her. I want her back."

Bruno narrows his eyes at me, and he takes my shoulder again.

"Sean, I love you like a brother. But you fuck with that woman again, and I will rip your balls off."

His fierce protectiveness is terrifying. I'd hate to get on the wrong side of Bruno, but I'm glad Gina has him in her corner.

"I don't intend on hurting her again."

"Good." He pushes his chair back and stands up. "But unless you're planning on sticking around for good, you leave her alone."

Bruno strides across the clubhouse, leaving me feeling like a pile of shit.

I hurt the only woman I've ever loved, and now I'm back here looking for a second chance. Even I know she'd be crazy to give me one.

3
GINA

Hot water cascades over my body. I've been in the shower so long that my fingertips are shriveled.

I tossed and turned all night thinking about Sean bloody O'Leary. It's both amazing and annoying that after all these years the way he says my name in his Irish lilt can still have an effect on me. My body's been on fire ever since he walked into the clubhouse last night. Strutted in smiling and teasing as if seven years hadn't passed.

Whenever I think about that cocky grin, wet heat surges between my legs.

God damn that man.

I fought the urge all night to reach for my Magic Wand. If I give in to getting myself off while fantasizing about Sean, it's one step closer to giving in to the real man.

But as the hot water falls on my nipples, making them pebble, I can't help running a hand over my breasts.

Promising myself I will definitely not think about Sean O'Leary, I slide my hands down my body, over my stomach to the sweet spot below.

My fingers press gently against the course hair, make little circles with my fingertips.

"Hello Gina." I can almost hear my name on his lips, and the thought makes my core tighten.

But I banish the memory from my mind. If I'm going to do this, I will not think about that man.

As my circles get firmer, his cocky smile and dancing eyes flash into my mind. I wonder if his long beard would scratch my thighs. I wonder if he still works out. I wonder if he has any new tattoos.

There was a time when I knew Sean's body as well as my own. And I wonder what it would be like to explore him again.

Dammit, I'm not going to think of Sean while I do this.

Feeling frustrated, I try to concentrate on myself. After seven years of being alone, I've gotten pretty good at self-love. One hand caresses my nipples, pinching them with the perfect amount of force.

But they turn into Sean hands, always rough with mechanic grease under his fingernails. I imagine them on me as I slide my finger between my wet folds.

The shrill ring of my phone pierces the air and pulls me out of my fantasy.

My eyes snap open and I'm back in the bathroom, just me with wrinkly fingers and my phone ringing. Disappointment and relief battle inside as the fantasy crashes around me.

Turning off the shower, I reach an arm out and grab my phone off the vanity. I'm expecting a call from the plumber today, and I don't want to miss it.

I'm expecting him to tell me I can move back into my apartment. But that's not why he's calling. They've hit a pipe. There's no damage, but it does mean there'll be no water for two days. Two more days before I can move back home.

Two more days, stuck here with Sean O'Leary in the room next to mine. That's the last thing I need.

I was hoping that putting some distance between us would calm this turmoil that's been inside of me ever since he strode through the clubhouse door. But I'll have to stick it out for a few more days.

As long as I can avoid him and his cocky grin, I'll be fine.

I step out of the shower and grab my towel. It's a small bathroom, and I'm a big woman. It takes a bit of gymnastics to shut the shower door and get myself dry.

I'm bent over with the towel between my toes when the door behind me opens.

I almost jump out of my skin. I was sure I locked that door, and now someone's getting a full view of my wide ass.

"Shit."

I straighten up, trying to wrap the towel around me, but it doesn't fit my substantial body.

From the low chuckle, I know before I turn around exactly who it is that's walked in on me.

"What the fuck are you doing in here?"

Sean's got one hand on the bathroom door as he watches me struggle to get the towel over my boobs while not showing off my lady parts. By the look on his face, he's obviously enjoying the show.

"I need a piss."

"Still so vulgar."

"Still so beautiful," he snaps back without missing a beat.

I try not to let the words affect me. Sean was always a charmer, but it's been a long time since anyone called me beautiful.

"I'm having a shower," I say indignantly, wanting to wipe that smirk of his face. "Didn't you hear the water running?"

"I just woke up, didn't hear a thing."

He's got a perpetually cocky grin, and it reminds me that I could never quite tell if he was joking or not. Or if what he was saying was the truth.

"I thought I locked that door."

"It was unlocked."

His face is a picture of innocence, which makes me suspicious. I wouldn't put it past Sean to pick the lock.

I pull the towel tighter around my chest, but that only makes it ride up my legs.

Sean's gaze travels to my exposed thighs, and he licks his lips.

He looks hungry, like a man who hasn't eaten in weeks looking at a juicy steak. That hungry look sends a thrill through my body and makes my core ache.

"You do look good, Gina." He takes a step toward me. "I wonder if you taste the same."

Damn his audacity. It has me clenching my thighs together as my body betrays every warning my mind is screaming at it.

I take a step back and bump up hard against the vanity.

"I've thought about you every day for the last seven years, Gina, wondering if I'll ever get a chance to kiss you again."

He takes another step forward, and I've got no place to go. His thighs bump against mine, and his hot breath skims my lips.

We're inches apart and I should push him away, but I'm also wondering if he tastes the same.

"It was a long shower, Gina. Makes me wonder what you were doing in there."

Oh fuck. Caught.

"I was washing my hair," I say quickly, but I can't meet his eye and my cheeks flush.

Sean gives a low chuckle, his eyes sparkling.

"Was it me you were thinking of Gina?"

He's as arrogant as I remember, and I'd love to wipe

that cocky grin right off his face. But I'd also like to grab that face and bury it between my legs.

Only a few inches separate us, and the heat between us is intense. It feels like my pussy is on fire.

If I hadn't been interrupted taking care of business, I'm sure I wouldn't feel this way. But I'm already horny and the way he's talking to me isn't helping, saying my name at every opportunity as if he knows what that does to me.

He takes a strand of wet hair between his fingers.

"I've never met anyone with this exact shade of hair, Gina. Gold, flecked with auburn."

He tucks the hair behind my ear, and God help me, my pussy gives an involuntary jerk at his touch.

I feel powerless to resist him. I feel like I'm twenty-four again and letting myself be seduced with sweet words and an Irish lilt.

I shouldn't do this, I really shouldn't. But as his mouth moves toward mine, I part my lips in anticipation.

Maybe it's because it's been seven years since a man touched me. Maybe it's because Sean's the only man that ever touched me. Or maybe it's because I've thought about Sean every day for the last seven years too. Whatever my reasons, when his lips press against mine, it's like fireworks going off over my whole body.

His mouth is soft and achingly familiar. An involuntary sigh escapes my lips. It feels so right, even though my head is telling me it's all wrong.

His kiss wakes up parts of me that have been sleeping

for seven years. With one kiss my body feels alive, every nerve ending on fire.

My nipples tingle, my toes curl, and my pussy practically purrs.

Sean cups my cheeks in his hands as he kisses me. His touch is gentle, so tender. It's everything I didn't know I was missing, and everything I can't let in.

I wrench myself from the kiss, pulling myself out of the sweetness of the moment, and I push him away.

I'm not that twenty-four-year-old girl anymore. I'm a woman who knows her mind. And I won't give into this base desire. Because that's all it is. A desire for something familiar, something nostalgic.

But I know how that ends, with Sean leaving and me left alone. Entirely alone.

"No, Sean, I'm not doing this."

"Gina, I've missed you so much. I never stopped loving you."

I hold up my hand, cutting him off. I don't want to hear his sweet talk; I don't want his Irish charm.

I spent too long building up my defenses. I'm annoyed that I let them down so easily, but it won't happen again.

"It was nice to kiss you, Sean. But it was a mistake."

"Not if it's what we both want."

"It's not what I want."

The disappointment on his face almost makes me waver, but he's probably just upset that he's not getting laid. I have to protect my own heart.

"Let me make myself clear, Sean. You broke my heart

once. I won't let it happen again. There is no chance of anything happening between us. Ever again."

Before he can say anything to change my mind, I exit the bathroom through the door that leads to my room and lock it firmly behind me.

I will not give myself to Sean O'Leary. Not my body and certainly not my heart.

4
SEAN

Gina's lips are as soft as I remember, her kisses as tender. There's a lot of heart in that woman, and she kisses with a passion that drives me nuts.

It's obvious that there's something still between us that she's denying. Did I really hurt her so much that she can't even stand to be in a room with me for more than a few minutes?

I hated to leave the way I did seven years ago. But she has to understand that there was nothing else I could do.

If I could have taken her with me, I would have, but it was too dangerous. I thought she'd understand. I thought she might have forgiven me, but she obviously hasn't.

It just means I have to work all the harder to win her over.

I slip the bobby pin out of my pocket and chuck it in the trash. Yeah, I picked the lock. She was right about that. But I wasn't going to pass up an opportunity to get a sneak peek of the woman I love in the shower. I've fantasized about that exact scenario too many times.

There's a painful ache in my cock, and I adjust my trousers. It's not going to get any better while the image of Gina in a towel is emblazoned in my mind.

She's a hell of a woman. She's filled out and it suits her, although I think it's mostly the way she's unapologetic about her size. Her confidence is sexy as hell. Always was, still is.

But it's not just her body I want. It's Gina's heart that I need to win over.

If I know my girl, she'll be angry with herself for letting me kiss her, even though I could tell it was exactly what she wanted.

I grab my bike and head out along the coast. It's a short drive to Gina's house, but I have business with her plumber. I slip him a brown envelope full of with cash and check that the pipe he broke isn't doing any real damage.

Yeah, that was me too. I have to keep her close to me a little longer.

It's a little cocky, but I've never shied away from being cocky to get what I want. And Gina is the only thing I want.

The plumber bought me some time with Gina. Now I have to make the most of it.

. . .

A few hours later, I'm back at the clubhouse.

I find Gina in the office, a spreadsheet open on the computer. She manages the admin side of the club now, and I feel a surge of pride for her.

I knock quietly on the door.

"I bought you a peace offering." I hold up a brown paper bag, and Gina narrows her eyes suspiciously.

"I won't try to kiss you again. I promise."

I'm pleased to see a flicker of disappointment cross her face.

"And not walk in on me in the shower. Can you promise me that?"

"I'll try my best, but you really should lock the doors."

She looks at me sharply as if she knows I'm lying about the door, but I give her a grin and hold out the bag.

"Are cinnamon donuts still your favorite?"

Her smile tells me all I need to know. She opens the bag and closes her eyes as the smell of baked cinnamon wafts out.

"Still my favorite."

Her moan when she bites into one sends my blood heading south, but she seems to have no idea how she's affecting me.

"What are you doing this afternoon?"

She looks at me like I'm stupid. "Working."

"Bruno said you can have the afternoon off."

She folds her arms across her chest and eyes me warily. "Did he now?"

"Yeah, said he wants you to go on a ride with me. Thinks you need some fresh air."

I'm bullshitting, and she knows it. But she tilts her head back and laughs.

"You're such a liar, Sean."

I laugh with her, because it feels so fucking good.

"Let's get away from this place, Gina. For a few hours, just you and me, somewhere where we can talk."

"We've got nothing to talk about, Sean. It's in the past."

"I want to explain. Clear the air about what happened."

She hesitates, and I can tell I'm getting through to her. Her good nature is winning out over her misgivings about me.

"Give me a couple of hours, and then I'll never bother you again if that's what you want."

She stands up with a sigh."

"All right, Sean. You've got an hour."

I try not to grin like a maniac. I've got an hour to convince Gina not to hate me.

My Fat Boy's parked out front. It was the first thing I bought when I got back to the States. Gina smiles when she sees it.

"Still like Harleys."

"Always."

I hand her a helmet, and she slides on behind me.

"You better put your arms around me, love."

"I'll hold on to the seat."

She always was a stubborn one. But at least she's on the back of my bike, where she belongs.

We pull out of the club complex and onto the ocean road.

With the salt wind whipping at my face and Gina's warm body pressed behind me, I feel happy for the first time in seven years.

5
GINA

Wind whips at my hair, sending it trailing behind me under the helmet.

As we turn the corners of the coastal highway, it's hard not to bump up against Sean. I allow myself, just for a moment, to rest against his back, to breathe in his scent of leather and the ocean. To remember what it was like to be young and carefree on the back of his bike, with our whole future ahead of us, feeling like the world was ours for the taking and nothing could ever separate us.

How naive we were.

We drive along the coastal highway to Temptation Bay. There's a little café, and I stop to say hi to Mira, admiring her round belly and the little boy clinging to her skirt.

If there's a twinge of envy at her pregnant belly, I don't let it show. I've had practice at keeping my regret to myself.

When I swore off men, I knew the decision I was making. I'll never be a mother. But there are enough babies around the clubhouse these days that I can be the cool aunt who spoils them rotten.

Sometimes when I watch Valentine or Scarlett breastfeeding, looking down at their babies with such wonder, I feel a yearning so deep in my belly that I almost can't breathe and have to leave the room. But everyone has disappointments in life. I don't let mine show.

We take our fish and chips and walk past the marina and over the rocks to the sand dunes. Sean tells me about his mother and Ireland and the business they were running. He still has the power to make me laugh with anecdotes about being chased by angry goats when he was hiding out in a field once.

We take a seat amidst the dunes and unfold the newspaper that holds the fish and chips. They're nice and greasy, the batter crunchy at the edges just the way I like them.

It doesn't take long to polish off the fish and pick our way through the chips.

"You know why I left," says Sean, suddenly turning serious. "You know why I had to go so suddenly and why I couldn't take you with me, don't you, Gina?"

I know the whole story. It was a tough time for the club. There was trouble with The Reapers, and they were out for retaliation. A body was found with Sean's DNA all over it. It was planted by the Reapers, but we had no way to prove it.

We got a tip-off from the police chief, who's an old school friend of Bruno's. The cops were coming to arrest Sean, and with the false evidence stacked against him, it didn't look good. He was looking at a life sentence.

The club smuggled him out before the police turned up.

Sean had to skip the country. He's been hiding in Ireland under a false name and passport, pretending to be an employee of his mother's business, not her son.

Recently, Bruno was finally able to provide enough evidence to prove who had really committed the murder.

The charges were finally dropped against Sean, meaning he could return to the States without fear.

I know he had no choice except to leave. But it didn't make it hurt any less.

"I would have gone with you, Sean," I tell him now. "I would have followed you anywhere."

It feels easy talking to him like this, in the past tense, as if it's a different girl I'm talking about, and in a way it is.

"I know, love. But the Reapers were out to get me. They've got a branch in Ireland. It was too dangerous. I went from safe house to safe house for a long time. I wanted you there, Gina, you have to believe me. But I couldn't put your life in danger. It was the hardest thing I've ever done, leaving like that without saying goodbye. Bruno promised to explain it to you. And I thought with the letters... I don't know what I thought..."

He trails off and I look out to the ocean, thinking about all the things that might have been.

"It doesn't matter now, Sean. It's in the past."

"But I want to apologize, Gina. I never said I'm sorry. That matters to me."

He takes my hands in his. It's not often that Sean gets serious, and when he does it's intense. He's looking at me now pleading for forgiveness.

I search my heart. I understand why he left that way; I really do. It's what came after that still hurts, but that's not his fault.

"I forgive you, Sean."

He smiles sadly, and I wonder if he's thinking about how our lives could have been if he's stayed.

"Remember how we used to come out here in the dunes?" A wicked glint comes into his eyes. "That night you were knocking back the whiskey."

I snort laugh at him, all indignant. "I was not. I remember you were knocking it back. I was trying to stop you."

"Well, someone drunk a whole hipflask, and I'm sure it wasn't just me."

We used to lay a blanket down in the dunes and talk about the cottage we'd buy by the ocean and the family we'd fill it with. Then we'd make love under the stars.

The memory makes me flush with heat.

We were reckless in those days, careless. Driving after a few drinks, making love without protection. I thought Sean would be here forever.

I was stupid. I was naive.

The memory chills me and I stand up abruptly, brushing sand off my jeans.

"I need to get back."

I can't go down this memory lane. Not now.

I leave Sean staring after me as I stride back to the road.

6
SEAN

Every time I feel like I'm making progress with Gina, I say something stupid and it pushes her away even further.

I thought bringing her back here to the place where we were so happy might help us reconnect, but it's only made her more distant.

I find her leaning against the bike, her arms folded and her mouth drawn in a thin line. She looks cross, and I don't really understand why.

"What's the matter, love?"

"It's dragging up these old memories, Sean. There's no point to it. I've moved on."

Her words cut like a knife to the chest. Because I haven't moved on. I've spent seven years on the run and hiding, and the only thing that kept me going was the thought of coming back here and claiming my woman.

Although now that I'm here, I'm not doing a very good job of it.

"We've both moved on," she says.

She throws her arms up in frustration, and I have a realization: There's something I'm missing. Something happened that I don't know about.

"There's something else, isn't there?"

She looks away, and I know I'm right.

"What happened, Gina? Tell me. Maybe I can help fix it."

Gina stares out to sea for a long time, and I think she's going to talk. Instead she just shakes her head slightly.

"Take me back to the clubhouse, please."

I don't know what it is that's wrong with her, but it's eating me up inside. I know there's no point pushing, so reluctantly I drive her back, brooding the whole way.

As soon as I pull up outside the clubhouse, Gina's off the bike and crossing the pavement to get inside.

She passes Gage who holds a little bundle up to her, a wide grin on his face.

"Olive, meet Auntie Gina."

Gina gives the new baby a quick look but continues inside. Gage looks put out, but only for an instant. As soon as he sees me, he holds up the squirming bundle.

"This is my little girl," he says proudly.

I take the baby from his arms. Her pink skin is baggy like she hasn't grown into it yet, and her face is screwed up in a toothless wail. She's a shriveled up little thing, but the way Gage is looking at his newborn, you'd think she was the most beautiful creature alive.

I make cooing noises at the baby, but I'm distracted by Gina.

Gage has been around the club for a long time, and he and Gina went to school together. He knows her better than anyone.

"Do you know what happened, man? Do you know why Gina hates me so much?"

He gives me an odd look. "Aside from the fact that you broke her heart?"

I get the feeling not all of the guys have forgiven me for how I left Gina. Even if they understand why.

"Did something else happen, something I don't know about?"

If she hooked up with someone, I'll lose my mind.

He shakes his head slowly. "Nah, but she gave you the best years of her life." He says that like it should mean something, but I still don't understand.

He's always been smart, Gage. I'm not surprised to hear he writes books. Although I am mildly surprised to hear that he writes romance, or romantic suspense as he takes great pains to clarify.

"Ever since we were kids, Gina wanted babies. She's watched everyone around her start a family. She hides it well, but I imagine that's a hard thing to see."

The baby turns toward the sound of Gage's voice and reaches her tiny fingers out for him. I hand her back to her proud daddy, and suddenly I see how vulnerable that child is, how the scrunched up face is kind of cute.

Maybe that's what I took from Gina. The chance to have a family.

Well, if that's all it is, I can still give her babies. I can give her a whole house full of babies. We can start straight away.

"Thanks, man." I slap Gage on the back, but he's already looking lovestruck into the face of his baby girl.

I head to the bar, and there's a big lad with sandy blonde hair pouring himself a drink.

"You got any Irish whiskey?"

Lyle grins at me. He's one of the newer guys, ex-military, and seems like a solid sort.

"Bruno brought it in especially for you."

He pours out a glass and I knock it back, the fiery heat settling in my belly. Then I grab another glass and head upstairs.

I don't know if I'm smothering Gina. But I've waited too long for her, and I'm not going to give up easily.

I knock on the door, and after a few moments she opens up.

She sighs when she sees me, but the tension from earlier has left her.

"You don't give up do you, Sean?"

"I brought you a drink." I hold up the bottle and two glasses, giving her my best cocky grin.

She's got her hands on her hips and she eyes me

wearily, but then she crooks her head, indicating me to follow her inside the room.

These are the basic rooms of the clubhouse. There's just a bed and a little table with two chairs. I take a seat, and I pour out two glasses.

She knocks hers back quickly and almost chokes.

"Christ, I haven't had a whiskey in years."

"You want another?"

She hesitates before answering. "Go on then. The burn is nice."

I know what she means. There's nothing like whiskey to warm you up.

As she sips her second drink slowly, I watch her closely. There're lines around her eyes that weren't there before. The years have been kind to Gina, but they've also taken a toll. I detect a sadness about her.

I wait until she finishes her drink, and I pour the next one before I say what I came to ask. I figure if she's a little tipsy she might open up to me.

"Why did you not meet another man? I hate the thought of it, and it used to drive me wild with jealousy thinking about you being with someone else. But I also wanted you to be happy. I didn't want you to be alone."

She finishes her drink, and her cheeks have a pink flush to them.

"It was hard for me, Sean, when you left. I understand why you had to leave. I really do. These things come with club life. But that didn't make it any less painful. I didn't want to risk my heart again."

Something doesn't add up. Plenty of people get their hearts broken. Gina's a passionate woman. I can't believe she wouldn't want to find someone else, as much as I'm glad she didn't.

"You always wanted babies, Gina, and it saddens me that you haven't had that."

She looks up at me sharply, and there's pain behind her eyes. I put my hand gently on hers.

"Tell me what happened, love."

I move my thumb, gently tracing the delicate lines of her hand and willing her to open up. After a few moments, she lets out a long sigh as if bracing herself. She looks me in the eye, and there's sadness there, and pain.

"I was pregnant when you left, Sean."

The words are like a shock wave to my heart. I can only gape at her, speechless.

"A few days after you left, I found out I was pregnant."

I feel like I've been punched in the gut. Gina was pregnant, and I left her. The woman I love was pregnant, and I left. No wonder she hates me.

"Where's the baby?"

Gina shakes her head slowly, tears pooling in the corners of her eyes.

"I lost it, Sean. I miscarried. It bled right out of me."

Miscarried. The word is like a concrete block pushing on my chest. She went through this without me.

I push the chair back and pace the room.

"Why did no one tell me?" My MC brothers should have told me something like this.

"Because nobody knew. There was so much going on at that time. Everyone was worried about you. The cops were harassing us, the Reapers were on our asses. I wasn't going to bother anyone with my problems."

"Shit, Gina, I would have come back. I would never have left you alone with a baby."

"You would have ended up inside."

"I don't care. I would have been there for you."

She shakes her head sadly. "I know. That's why I didn't tell anyone. I was going to leave the club. Go away somewhere to have the baby. I knew if you knew about it, you'd come back for us. And that couldn't happen.

"The bleeding started one night when I was working the bar downstairs. I kept having to run to the bathroom and watch our baby bleed out down the toilet. Knowing I couldn't tell anyone, I stuffed a pad in my underwear and kept working. It was the worst night of my life."

The thought of Gina going through that alone makes my whole body feel heavy. I sink to my knees in front of her, trembling. Hating the fact that I was oblivious to it all.

"Didn't you tell anyone then, see a doctor?"

She shakes her head. "Women lose babies all the time, Sean. It was only about seven weeks along."

What she's telling me is devastating. The thought of Gina all alone and losing our baby makes my heart hurt in new ways.

"I'm so sorry I wasn't here for you, Gina. I'm so sorry you went through that alone. How about any of the other girls? Did you tell any of them?"

"There was no one I was close to. I'd been so caught up with you that I didn't have any female friends. I worked a lot because I was getting money together to run away, because I knew if anyone found out I was pregnant, they'd tell you and you'd come back for me."

She's not wrong. If I knew she was carrying my child, I would have moved heaven and earth to be here for her. I would have risked a life sentence for her.

Instead, Gina was alone, and she bled out our baby all alone.

"I'm so sorry this happened to you."

I enfold her in my arms, and she leans into me. I rub her back, wanting to comfort her, but it doesn't feel like enough. I'll never make up for not being there when she needed me.

"I was so lonely, Sean. I was so scared."

Her body starts to heave as tears fall down her cheeks.

All the years I've known Gina, I've never seen her cry. Now the tears slide down her cheeks, tears that she's kept back for the last seven years.

And they're not delicate tears either. They're big wracking sobs. Snot drips from her nose, and her mascara runs down her cheeks. It's messy and raw and makes me love her all the more.

"I'm so sorry," I whisper over and over again, knowing it will never be enough.

We don't talk anymore; I just hold her as she lets all the hurt and anguish out. Everything she's been holding inside for the last seven years.

I don't know if it's the whiskey, or the confession, or the hurt that's finally being shared, but eventually she sags against me, exhausted.

I help her into bed, peeling her shoes off and tucking her under the blankets.

"I'm glad you told me, love, and I'm so sorry. I can't change what's happened. But I can promise you that from now on you'll never be alone. I never stopped loving you, Gina. I thought about you every single day since I left. It's you I've come back for."

She squints up at me, her eyes raw from crying.

"Once I got over the shock of it and the pain and the heartache and the loss and the grief, I promised myself I'd never let a man get close to me again. It's too risky, to lose a man and a baby within a few weeks. I couldn't go through that again."

I hate that she made that vow to herself, that she was so damaged and broken. I take her hand in mine.

"I'll stick around, I promise. Now go to sleep."

Her eyes flutter shut, and she leans back on the pillow. I keep her hand in mine until her breathing gets steady and regular.

7
SEAN

Once Gina's breathing gets deep and regular, I unclasp her hand from mine and lay it gently on the bed. I'm almost to the door when she stirs behind me.

"Stay." Her voice comes out as a whisper so faint I almost miss it.

"I thought you were asleep."

"Stay with me."

Her arm is outstretched, reaching for me. She looks so vulnerable, and after what she's just told me, I don't blame her for not wanting to be alone.

"I'll stay as long as you want, love."

Slipping off my shoes, I slide onto the bed next to Gina and pull her toward me so her back's pressed against my chest. She feels familiar and yet different, her body fuller and more sensual.

I run my hand over her hair, smoothing down her locks and tucking them behind her ear. Her neck is exposed, and her soft skin is too tempting.

"Gina," My lips press against her neck. "It feels good to hold you in my arms again."

My kisses move down her spine as far as her t-shirt will allow me. I feel her shiver under my touch, and then she moves her hips against me.

It's a small movement and a big invitation.

I go instantly hard, but I don't want to take advantage of her when she's vulnerable. And so I pull back, putting some distance between us on the bed.

"Where are you going?"

She's wide awake now, and she rolls over to face me. We're closer now, more intimate.

"I'm sorry you went through all that on your own."

She screws her face up. "I don't want to talk about it anymore. I want to forget about it for a while."

Her eyes dart to my lips expectantly. I take her face in my hands and press my lips to hers.

She kisses me back, slow and tender. But she's vulnerable. I shouldn't take advantage, no matter how much I want to.

"Are you sure this is what you want, Gina? Because you spent a lot of time telling me that I'll never get to touch you again."

She sighs.

"No, I'm not sure at all, Sean. All I know is that ever

since you walked back into my life, my body has felt like it's on fire. And if I don't get a release soon, I think I might explode."

I know how she feels. I've felt the same thing ever since I saw her. But if she thinks this is just about sex, then she's crazy.

"I don't want to just be your release, Gina."

She chews on her lower lip, and I've never seen her look more vulnerable.

"I don't know, Sean, but right now I feel vulnerable and raw, and I want to feel something else. This might be a bad idea, but do you think for one night we can pretend we're those kids again?"

I want more than one night, but it's a start.

"I need this, Sean."

There's a pleading look in her eye, and who am I to turn down the love of my life begging me to make love to her?

"As long as you're certain."

My thumb grazes her cheek, wiping away smudged mascara.

"I need to confess something," she says quietly.

My gut clenches. This is where she tells me about the boyfriend she's been with for the past several years. So I do what I always do when I feel uneasy. I make a joke.

"Us Catholics love a good confession."

Her lips tug into a smile, and at least I've managed to cheer her up.

"I haven't been with a man since you."

The words send a new heat through my body. No other man has been inside her; it will be like claiming her all over again.

"Gina, you're driving me crazy."

"Just touch me, Sean. It means I've been horny for seven years, and I've not done anything about it."

I throw my head back and laugh. Gina always told me I was funny, but no one can make me laugh the way she does.

"I'll do more than touch you if that's what you want."

I kiss her eyelids, salty with the remnants of tears. Then I tenderly move down to her mouth. Her lips pressing against mine is everything I've imagined and more.

Her body moves against mine, finding the new places where we fit together.

It starts tender, but as we relax into each other, there's a new urgency to the kisses. I've fantasized about making love to Gina for so long, and now that she's here next to me, I need to touch all of her.

Pulling her t-shirt over her head, I unclip her bra.

Her magnificent breasts tumble out of the bra, and I take them in my hands, burying my head between them.

"I've missed these girls."

She gives a deep throaty laugh.

"They've missed you too, Sean."

I can tell by the hard nipples and her gentle sigh that she's telling me the truth. I suck on each one of them tenderly until she tilts my head up.

"Other parts of me have missed you too, Sean."

"Still bossy I see."

But I don't mind. Gina was never afraid to ask for what she wants and I love that, especially in the bedroom.

Trailing kisses over the soft rolls of her belly, I make my way down to her most tender spot.

She wiggles out of her panties and I bury my face between her legs, breathing in her tangy scent and tasting her sweet nectar. It feels good to be here, between her legs. This is what I was made for, giving Gina pleasure.

I take my time, licking slow circles on her hard nub, enjoying the way she squirms with every touch. I can feel the tension she's been holding onto, and I enjoy turning her into a quivering mess.

It doesn't take long until she releases it all, exploding on my tongue, pulling my hair and screaming my name. It's the sweetest sound I've ever heard.

I climb back up to her, grabbing a condom from my pocket as I kick my jeans off.

"You carry a condom?" She raises her eyebrows at me.

"I slipped this in my pocket the day I came back hoping I'd get this chance with you."

"That's very presumptuous."

"I call it confident." I give her my best grin, and she meets it with a sparkle in her eye. I love seeing Gina smile, but right now I want to see her screaming.

We kiss some more, and I roll my cock around the

edge of her pussy. She's wet and ready for me, and I slide in an inch.

She's so tight that when her pussy squeezes me I almost lose it. I remember our first time together, when I took her virginity on the sand dunes. The memory sends a spasm down my cock, and I jerk inside her.

"Fuuuck, it feels so good to be inside you, Gina."

"Go all the way, Sean." She's panting, and her face is slick with sweat. I thrust hard, burying my cock deep within her.

"Sean," she gasps, and I love the sound of my name on her lips. I want to hear that sound for the rest of my life.

I move slowly, wanting to treasure every moment. I've imagined making love to Gina so many times. At first, trying to remember every detail of every time we made love, and when the memories faded, fantasizing about her. But nothing on this earth compares to how it feels to be inside Gina. It's familiar and exciting all at once. It feels like coming home after a long exile.

We find a rhythm, moving together, our bodies entwined, locking and syncing like they were made for this. I rub circles around her clit with my thumb until her pants turn to screams and her pussy convulses around me. Only then do I let myself go and give in to the sensation of Gina's pussy clenched around my cock.

As my cum explodes into her, I feel a sense of wonder. My heart swells with love, full in a way that it hasn't been for so long.

We collapse onto the bed together, panting and exhausted.

I enfold Gina in my arms, and it doesn't take long until she's breathing heavily. I pull her close, wanting to feel her against me as I sleep. As I drift off, a deep feeling of contentment settles into my heart. It feels like finally I’ve come home.

8
GINA

My head's throbbing when I wake up, and my mouth's bone dry. I don't know if it's from the whiskey or dehydration from crying so much.

Telling Sean about the miscarriage was like a weight lifting off my shoulders, and making love to him felt like part of that release.

It was lovely and tender and everything I remember. I feel lighter and like maybe, just maybe, there's a chance for us.

I roll over, wanting to snuggle into him, but the other side of the bed's empty.

"Sean?"

I lift myself onto my elbows so I can see all the corners of the room. But he's not there. I try not to be disappointed; he must have gotten up before me is all.

My phone pings with an incoming message and I grab my phone eagerly, hoping it's Sean. But it's from

Gage asking if I'm coming down to the office today. We're meant to be going over the accounts.

I check the time and gasp when I see it's almost 10 o'clock. I never sleep this late, ever.

I send Gage a quick reply and head to the bathroom.

Sean must have slipped out and left me sleeping. I ignore the niggling feeling in the pit of my stomach. I'm sure there's an explanation.

There's a glass on the vanity and I take a long drink of water, the cool liquid soothing my throat and clearing my head.

I haven't cried like that in years. I haven't allowed myself to. I feel lighter. I didn't know how good it would feel to share that burden. To tell Sean about the baby and about the loss. To collapse into his arms and let him soothe me.

No one has cared for me like that in a long time. I'm usually the one caring for everybody else. It felt so nice to share my burden, to have someone look after me for once.

I put the glass down and stare at my reflection in the mirror. I barely recognize myself. Mascara lines stain my cheeks, and my eyes are clogged with gunk from all those tears.

I push my fingers up my cheeks, moving the skin of my face around. There're lines around my mouth that weren't there a few years ago and a darkness that's perpetually smudged under my eyes.

When did I get so old looking?

I turn my head from side to side, looking for the carefree girl I used to be. Somewhere over the years, she vanished inside of me. I'll be thirty-four next month, and it feels like life is passing me by.

But maybe it doesn't have to be that way.

Maybe Sean coming back is a second chance. A chance to have all those things I dreamed of when I was a young girl. A good man, a home of our own, and lots of babies.

Plenty of women have children later in life these days. Thirty-four isn't too old, is it?

But I'm getting ahead of myself. It was one night with Sean, and I'm already planning a family with him.

I laugh at myself, but I can no longer deny the feelings I have for Sean. The feelings that I've always had for him.

Maybe, just maybe, it's worth taking another risk. Because otherwise I'm going to be looking in the mirror in another seven years wondering what could have been.

I have a quick shower and throw on some clothes. Now that I've made up my mind, I want to tell Sean, tell him that I do want to give us another chance. That I think we can make it this time.

Sean's room is the one next to mine, and I knock softly on the door. When there's no answer, I knock again, louder this time. When there's still no answer, I push open the door.

"Sean?"

Light streams in the window, and the bed's made up neatly. There're no bags. There's no clothing strung over the chair. Or any sign of Sean. I try the door to the shared bathroom, but he's not in there. I even open the door on the other side that leads through to my room.

But he's gone. Sean's gone, and so have his bags.

I sink onto the bed. What a fool I've been. I let him charm me again, won over by his kind words and cocky smile. And now he's got what he wanted and he's left.

Fresh tears sting my eyes, but I don't let them fall. I won't cry for him anymore.

I can't believe I've been so foolish a second time.

I spend the rest of the day catching up on work in the clubhouse. Sean's not there either. And Gage tells me he saw him leaving this morning, and he hasn't been back.

I try to convince myself that he's not left for good, that he wouldn't do that to me again. But no one knows where he's gone.

I get a call from the plumber to tell me that the water's back on. I don't feel like hanging around the clubhouse, so once we've finished with the accounts, I pack my bags and head back to my place.

My apartment feels empty after the hustle and bustle of the clubhouse. I drop my keys on the counter, letting the silence engulf me.

I wasn't made to live alone. I like being surrounded by people. But somehow, life doesn't always turn out how you want.

I check the cupboards and find instant noodles

stuffed at the back. A single woman's pantry. But I don't have any groceries, and I don't feel like cooking anyway.

I'm making a cup of tea when I hear the sound of a bike. My stupid heart thumps louder in my chest when I see it's Sean.

I pull open the door just as he reaches my doorstep, blocking his way with my body. I'm not going to let him come inside and fool me again. I'll not fall for his Irish charm and cocky grin.

"I'm sorry I wasn't around today, Gina." He's smiling, and I have to look away or I'm going to get taken in by his easy good looks. "I had something important to do."

"You've always got something important to do, Sean."

It comes out bitter, and he takes a step back.

"There's nothing more important to me than you, Gina. Now that I'm back, I intend to stay."

I eye him warily, not sure what I can believe anymore.

"Why did you take off this morning, Sean? Why haven't you messaged me all day?"

I hate the way I'm sounding like a nag, but after our history, I can't help myself.

"I've got a surprise for you."

"I've had enough surprises, Sean. I can't take this yo-yo-ing. Either you're here or you're not. I'm too old to play games."

He puts his hands on my shoulders, and his touch is reassuring. But I step away. I cannot let this man get to me again.

"I am one hundred percent here, Gina. And I know

it's hard for you to believe me, so I want to show you something."

He holds out a hand, and God help me, I take it. Maybe I'm stupid, but I want to believe in him so much that I want to believe that he's going to stay. But it's so hard for me to.

He leads me down the stairs to his bike.

"Are you going to take me to the dunes and try and seduce me again?"

"Would you be open to it?" he asks cockily.

My eyes are rolling before I can stop them. I should have known better than to get a serious answer out of him.

"Get on the bike, Gina. I've got something to show you. And then if you don't want me, I'll disappear. You'll never hear from me again."

"I wish I'd never laid eyes on you in the first place."

But I'm joking, slipping into the easy banter we've always shared. Whatever happens between us, my time with Sean has always been the best time in my life. When I've felt the most awake, the most alive.

Not knowing if I'm leading myself to more heartbreak, I get on the back of the bike.

As we head out of town, I slide my arms around Sean's waist and hold him tight. It feels too good, and I lean my head against the back of him. Even if it's the last time I do it, I vow I will enjoy this ride.

We take the Pacific Highway, and this time we go up the coast. There's a little bay we used to come to when we were together. We used to dream about owning one of the cottages there. The perfect place to start a family, close to the ocean and close to the road, the two things that the both of us love.

We turn in there now, and Sean slows the bike.

There's a row of houses along the beach, and we pull up in front of one that has a for sale sign out front.

"Come on." He slides off the bike. "The real estate agent told me where to find the key."

"You've already looked at this?"

A kernel of excitement unfurls in my stomach. Why is Sean showing me this house?

"Stop asking questions, Gina. Just come with me and tell me if you like it."

I already know I like it. It's perfect. My dream home, with a white brick wall out front and large shady orange trees in the garden. Honeybees buzz around a bright flower garden, and the scent of lavender hangs on the air.

Sean squeezes my hand as he walks me up to the front porch. He takes a key from under a potted plant and lets us in.

Polished wooden floorboards run all the way to an open plan living room and kitchen area, with French doors that lead out the back of the house to a large deck and backyard. Beyond the yard, there's a path through the trees that leads to the sand dunes and ocean beyond.

I always wanted to live by the seaside. I can see us living here. A big yard for the kids, a walk to the beach.

My heart's racing with excitement, and I need some answers.

"Why are you showing me this place?"

"I'm thinking about buying it."

"You can't be serious."

"I've never been more serious. Do you like it, Gina? Could you live here?"

We're on the deck now and I grab hold of a wooden chair, needing to ground myself.

I can imagine what it would be like watching our kids play in the garden. Coming back from the beach sunburned with salt on our skin.

"It's like we always dreamed about. A little cottage by the ocean. Just you and me. And our ten children."

I snort laugh and turn to face him, ready to make some smartass remark, but my voice catches in my throat. Sean's down on one knee, holding up a little box.

"Gina, we've wasted too much time and I don't intend to waste another minute. Will you marry me?"

He tilts the box up, and it's the most beautiful ring I've ever seen. A string of blood red rubies with a diamond in the center. But it's not the ring I care about. It's the man that's holding it. The man that my heart sings for, the man I never stopped loving.

The man who broke me once but still is everything to me. The man who has the power to give me everything I've ever wanted. A family, the house, but the most important thing is him. Only we're not young anymore. Things are different now.

"I'll be thirty-four next month, Sean. I don't know if I can still give you children."

I twist my hands nervously, not wanting to look at him. "A woman's fertility tapers off; it might be too late…"

Sean shakes his head, exasperated.

"Gina. You're all I need. Of course, I'd love to have a family with you. But you, just you, are enough."

Tears sting my eyes, and my heart opens. I think about Sean and me when we were younger, how much in love we were. I think about the loss of the baby and the heartache and loneliness of the last seven years. And I think about the last few days, and how my body and soul have felt alive in a way that I had forgotten they could, in a way that I never thought I'd feel again.

"Yes, Sean. Yes, I'll marry you."

"Thank fuck for that, because my knees are killing me. You're not the only one getting old, love."

I'm laughing as he slides the ring on my finger and stands up, pulling me into his arms.

"Do you like the house?"

"It's perfect. Absolutely perfect."

"Good, because I've already put the deposit down."

"You have not."

"I have. Moved my stuff in and all. It's vacant, so I thought it wouldn't hurt to spend a few nights here."

I slap him playfully. That's the cocky man I know and love.

He spins me toward him and pulls me close so our bodies are pressed together.

"Well, this family isn't going to make itself. We'd better get started, especially as you've just pointed out that there's not a moment to lose."

"Sean, we can't do it here. This isn't our house."

"It will be soon. But you're right." I squeal as his scoops me up into his arms. "I'd better take you to the dunes."

I'm a big girl and he staggers, making us both laugh.

"Do you want me to walk?"

"No. A man should be able to carry his future wife."

I giggle as he sways and lurches under my weight. He's panting hard when we reach the beach, and we both collapse onto the sand laughing.

It's a quiet cove with a handful of houses surrounding it. There's no one around, but he pulls me into a dip in the dunes where no one can see us, just in case.

He kisses me then. It's a full and passionate kiss awakening a deep yearning inside of me. Our bodies may be a bit older and creakier and our hearts a little scarred, but that just adds to the deep love we feel for each other.

Sean pulls his t-shirt off and lays it on the sand like a blanket. We tug off each other's clothes until we're both naked, enjoying the feel of the sun and cool sea breeze on our bare skin.

I straddle him and take my time sliding him slowly inside of me. As I sink down onto him, I feel a sense of peace that I haven't felt in a long time. I can finally put the past behind me.

He clasps my cheeks in his hands and we look into each other's eyes, really seeing each other.

"I love you Gina, and this time I will never let you go."

"I love you too, Sean."

We make love slowly with the sound of the ocean breaking around us and the salt air gently skimming our bodies until we're overcome with our needs, panting together until we both reach a climax. My nails dig into his shoulder as I try not to scream and give away our position in the dunes.

Lying on the sand afterwards, I feel something else I haven't felt in a long time. Hope. Hope for our future together, hope for this exciting adventure that we're going on.

I'm opening my heart for the man that I love. That comes with a risk, but you don't get anything in life without risk. And this time, I know we'll make it.

EPILOGUE

GINA

Seven years later…

"Mind your sister," Sean calls to the boys.

They're on the trampoline, the three of them. The oldest, Kier at six, is the gentle one. He holds Niamh's chubby hands while she stares up at him, her expression going from cautious to wonder.

My little girl's only just learned to walk, and every time they bounce, she tumbles into her big brother. He catches her and she giggles at him, the same cocky grin as her father.

Liam, our five-year-old, bounces around them, oblivious to his little sister. He's the complete opposite of Kier, as wild and cocky as his father.

It's been seven years since I let Sean back into my life. And I've not regretted a single moment.

We got married in a small ceremony, and I was pregnant before we even moved into our house. So much for declining fertility. Kier and Liam were born only twelve months apart. They used to call that Irish twins, which is quite fitting.

But it took almost four years after that to get pregnant with Niamh.

It's not for lack of trying. We haven't used contraception since the night Sean proposed to me. I'll be turning forty next month, and I don't know if fate has any more children in store for me.

We once dreamed about a big family, but if three is what we end up with, I am more than happy with that.

"You want another drink, love?"

Without waiting for an answer, Sean pours me a glass of wine.

I've been at the clubhouse for most of the day getting the accounts ready with Gage. The two boys are at school, so Niamh comes in with me and Valentine or Scarlett looks after her while I work. I must be the luckiest working mom around. I get to sneak out and give her cuddles anytime I want.

Sean was welcomed back as a member. We spend half our time there with our extended family. I love my club brother and sisters, but I've got my own little family to take care of now.

There's nothing nicer than coming back to our place at the end of the day. Sitting on the back deck with a glass of wine and the smell of barbeque in the air, the sound of the ocean and watching the kids play with Sean by my side.

It's a life I never thought I'd have seven years ago. It's amazing the difference another seven years can make.

I have my cottage by the ocean. I have my three children. But best of all I have my husband.

Sean puts his hands on my shoulders and kisses the top of my head. His finger traces the line of my neck and I tilt my head, enjoying his touch.

"What are you doing later, Mrs. O'Leary?"

He kisses the back of my neck, making goosebumps appear on my arms.

"Probably just the dishes."

He chuckles, and his breath against my skin makes my nipples pebble. "Not if I have anything to do with it."

He straightens up. "Kids! Dinner's ready. And then it's straight to bed for you lot."

Kier helps Niamh off the trampoline, but Liam lets out a long moan.

"I want to stay up."

"You got school in the morning," says Sean, "And your mother and I need some alone time," he says so only I can hear.

The children come racing over, and Niamh opens her chubby arms to me.

"Momma, momma."

I scoop her up, planting kisses on her soft cheeks. She smells like freshly cut grass and sunshine. The boys are so much like their father, but my little girl is all mine.

She takes a sausage in her chubby hand, and I plunk her down at the table and squirt a generous helping of ketchup on her plate. She smears it on her sausage and all over her summer dress.

The boys argue over who's got the biggest burger while Sean sings an Irish ditty to drown them out and make everyone laugh.

It's noisy and it's messy. But it's my family life, and I love it.

It's the life I never thought I'd have. And every day I'm so thankful for giving Sean a second chance.

Sometimes you've got to risk your heart. You might get hurt, or you might end up like me, with everything you ever wanted.

WHAT TO READ NEXT

ALL THE SCARS WE CANNOT SEE

Man is not meant to live alone. He becomes dangerous, possessive, protective of what's his. And she is all mine...

Since retiring from the military, I don't like human company.

Until I meet Emily, my new neighbor.

She's as damaged as I am and running from her own demons.

When they catch up with her, I must fight my own inner darkness to protect the woman I love.

But two broken hearts don't always make a whole...

All the Scars We Cannot See is an instalove mountain man romance featuring a scarred ex-military recluse and a curvy girl on the run who steals his heart.

Keep reading for an exclusive excerpt or visit:
mybook.to/AllTheScarsWeCannotSee

ALL THE SCARS WE CANNOT SEE

CHAPTER ONE

Sam

Dust kicks up from the gravel and swirls around the car as it makes its way along the access road. Burgundy red Corolla. Early model hatchback with a dent in the passenger side door and one side mirror hanging off. It's barely roadworthy and certainly not the kind of vehicle suitable for the roads this far up the mountain.

Picking up my binoculars, I try to make out the driver. Through the dust haze, I can tell they're a woman with long dark hair and wearing wide sunglasses.

Probably a lost tourist out looking for an adventure off the beaten track. Only the back seat is loaded with belongings, making the back end of the car sag under the weight.

She must be lost. There's only my place and the abandoned farm up this road. It's the reason I bought this cabin. No neighbors. No tourists. Just me and the mountain.

Until this beat-up little car turned up on my access road.

I guess she'll figure out soon enough that this road doesn't lead anywhere. Then she'll turn around and go home.

Even as I'm thinking it, the car starts to slow down. It turns into the driveway to the abandoned farm. She'll turn around there and head back the way she came, back to the tourist trails where she belongs.

Only she doesn't. The car turns all the way into the driveway and stops just outside the farmhouse.

The driver's door opens, and a pair of long, thick legs step out. I adjust the focus on the binoculars to take her in.

She's got her back to me, giving a good view of her curvy hourglass figure, wide hips encased in ass-hugging leggings, and long dark hair hanging over her shoulders.

My blood rushes to my dick, and it's suddenly hard to breathe.

"Damn."

I pull the binoculars off my eyes and turn my head away, trying to get my racing pulse under control. It's been a long time since a woman had that kind of effect on me. Not that I get the chance to see many women these days.

Running a hand through my hair, I take a swig of the cool beer sitting next to me on the coffee table.

It does nothing to quench my thirst.

As soon as I raise the binoculars and train them on the woman, my throat goes bone dry.

Her hips sway as she walks to the front door of the house. That old farm has been empty since I moved in three years ago, so if she's expecting to call on someone, she'll be disappointed.

But she doesn't ring the bell. Instead she reaches for her keys and jiggles the lock. A moment later, she pushes open the front door and disappears into the house.

"Damn," I mutter for the second time as I lower the binoculars.

Looks like I got myself a new neighbor.

To keep reading visit:
mybook.to/AllTheScarsWeCannotSee

GET YOUR FREE BOOK

Sign up to the Sadie King mailing list for a FREE book!

You'll be the first to hear about new releases, exclusive offers, bonus content and all my news. You can even email me back. I love chatting with my readers!

To claim your free book visit:
www.authorsadieking.com/free

ALSO AVAILABLE IN PAPERBACK BY SADIE KING

Wild Heart Mountain

Military Heroes

Kobe brings together a group of military veterans who live on the side of Wild Heart Mountain. Can these wounded warriors find love or do their scars cut too deep?

Wild Riders MC

This group of ex-military bikers fall hard and fall fast when they encounter the curvy women who heal their hearts.

Mountain Heroes

Steamy stories featuring the men and women from Wild Heart Mountain's Search and Rescue and Fire service.

Sunset Coast

Underground Crows MC

Short and steamy MC romance stories of obsessed men and curvy girls.

Sunset Security

A security firm run by ex-military men who become obsessed with their curvy girls.

Filthy Rich Love

Bad boy billionaires of the Sunset Coast and young innocent curvy woman.

His Christmas Obsession

A Christmas romance about an obsessed biker who rides across the country in the snow to reach Cleo before he's even met her.

Men of the Sea

Super short and steamy tales from Temptation Bay of bad boys and curvy girls.

Love and Obsession

A bad boy trilogy featuring a thief, a henchman and an ex-military hitman who finds redemption with his curvy girl.

For a full list of Sadie King's books check out her website

www.authorsadieking.com

ABOUT THE AUTHOR

Sadie King is a USA Today Best Selling Author of short instalove romance.

She lives in New Zealand with her ex-military husband and raucous young son.

When she's not writing she loves catching waves with her son, running along the beach, and good wine, preferably drunk with a book in hand.

Keep in touch when you sign up for her newsletter. You'll even snag yourself a free short romance!

www.authorsadieking.com/free

www.ingramcontent.com/pod-product-compliance
Ingram Content Group UK Ltd.
Pitfield, Milton Keynes, MK11 3LW, UK
UKHW040012200726
13854UKWH00001B/159

9 798215 368022